BEHIND THE SCREEN

MASON FALLS MYSTERIES
BEHIND THE SCREEN

ISRAEL KEATS

MINNEAPOLIS

Darby Creek
A division of Lerner Publishing Group, Inc.
241 First Avenue North
Minneapolis, MN 55401 USA

For reading levels and more information, look up this title at www.lernerbooks.com.

Cover and interior images: iStock.com/Vectorfactory; AlenKadr/Shutterstock.com; iStock.com/Prykhodov; iStock.com/imagotres; iStock.com/Artizarus.

Main body text set in Janson Text LT Std 12/17.5.
Typeface provided by Adobe Systems.

Library of Congress Cataloging-in-Publication Data

Names: Keats, Israel, author.
Title: Behind the screen / Israel Keats.
Description: Minneapolis : Darby Creek, [2018] | Series: Mason Falls mysteries | Summary: When high school sophomore Hannah discovers that her sister Alexis, a senior, is involved with someone she met online, Hannah tries to learn if it is a scam.
Identifiers: LCCN 2017030499| ISBN 9781541501140 (lb) | ISBN 9781541501157 (pb) | ISBN 9781541501164 (eb pdf)
Subjects: | CYAC: Sisters—Fiction. | Online dating—Fiction. | Identity—Fiction. | Family life—Fiction. | Mystery and detective stories.
Classification: LCC PZ7.1.K396 Beh 2018 | DDC [Fic]—dc23

LC record available at https://lccn.loc.gov/2017030499

Manufactured in the United States of America
1-43786-33638-8/30/2017

TO JANE

CHAPTER 1

Hannah searched through the freezer. She wanted waffles, but all she could find were ice cubes and bags of vegetables. She dug deeper. She and her sister had just spent a week with their dad, but she was sure there were waffles before she left, and her mom and stepdad never ate frozen waffles.

"I need the fridge, Hannah," Alexis said behind her. Hannah shut the door and stepped out of the way. Alexis grabbed the soy milk and took it to the table. She held the milk in one hand and her phone in the other, thumb-typing a message.

"Who are you talking to?" Hannah asked. "You're not back together with Chris, are you?" Her big sister had broken up with her long-time boyfriend a few months ago. For a while she'd been really upset about it. She would lock herself in her room for hours and tear up at almost anything. But lately she been happy again. And she'd been on her phone a lot more.

"No!" said Alexis. "It's just a friend."

Hannah gave up on the waffles and looked in the fridge. She found a plastic tub of leftover pie and brought it to the table. She wasn't sure where the pie had come from. Her mom and stepdad must have had some while she and Alexis were at their dad's.

Alexis saw her with the pie and rolled her eyes.

"What?" Hannah asked. "This pie is mostly fruit. It's a good breakfast."

"Sure it is," said Alexis.

"Oh, good. You're both up!" their mother said as she came in. "I thought you might need help rolling out of bed since it's the first day after the winter break." She went to the coffee maker. "So, Hannah, have you given any thoughts to what you'll do the second half of your junior year?"

"Um. Go to school? Do homework?" Hannah said between bites.

"I mean besides that," her mother said. She spooned some coffee into the machine. "Maybe you could run for a student council position? I think the elections are in March."

"I don't think so," Hannah replied. "I don't like politics."

"Well, you're a computer whiz," their mom said. "Is there some kind of computer club?"

"Probably, but I'm not into them that much," Hannah said.

"Well, you should join something," their mother said. "Good grades aren't enough to get you into a top-notch college anymore. Tell her, Alexis."

Alexis snorted with laughter. Hannah looked over in surprise. Alexis wasn't laughing at their mom, she was laughing at something on her phone.

"Alexis?" their mother said again. "Tell Hannah how your involvement got you accepted at Bailey. You're on student council, and you started that future women leaders group."

Alexis set the phone aside. "Well, I'm me and Hannah is Hannah," she said slowly.

Hannah wasn't sure what Alexis meant by that comment, but she got the feeling it wasn't meant in a nice way. *Typical Alexis*, thought Hannah. *She always thinks she's so much better than me.*

Hannah glanced at Alexis's phone and saw a handsome guy's picture attached to the last message: big smile, nice teeth, good haircut. *So this just-a-friend is a guy.* Hannah could also see his last text to Alexis: *I can't wait to meet IRL.*

I don't know why she'd spend so much time texting a guy she hasn't actually met in person, but something tells me this is more than a friend, Hannah thought.

/////

Alexis drove them both to school. She'd gotten a car when she turned eighteen. It was small and old but reliable, even on cold January mornings.

Alexis's phone buzzed before they even got to the first stop sign. Alexis glanced at it, and

Hannah knew she was dying to check her latest message. But she was good about staying off the phone while driving.

In fact, until recently Alexis hadn't been so attached to her phone at all. Hannah thought hard. When had this texting frenzy started? Before Thanksgiving, she remembered, because they'd gone to their dad's house the next day and he was mad that Alexis spent the whole time staring at her screen. But it started *after* Halloween because she and Alexis had handed out candy and neither of them stopped to check their phones then.

The phone buzzed again. Alexis almost reached for it but stopped herself.

"Do you want me to read the message to you?" Hannah asked.

"No, of course not," Alexis waved her hand like she was shooing a fly. "I can wait until we're stopped." They reached the school. Alexis crawled through the big, packed lot in search of a spot.

For the last couple of months, Hannah had assumed Alexis was texting with a bunch of different friends. Getting back into things after the breakup. Gossiping, making plans, talking about her school activities and assignments.

Now Hannah wondered if most—or even all—of the texts were with this mysterious guy.

/////

Alexis gave her rides in the morning, but Hannah usually had to catch the bus home because Alexis had activities or a study group after school. On the ride home that afternoon, Hannah looked through a list of extracurricular activities that she'd gotten from the office.

"Hey, Hannah. Whatcha doin'?" Jacob nudged her. She slid over so he could sit down. Back in middle school, they'd gotten together regularly to play video games with some other kids. Their group had sort of fizzled out in high school. She and Jacob had stayed friends, but this was the first time she'd seen him since the start of winter break.

"Thinking about signing up for something," she told him.

"Really?"

"Really! Why is that such a shock?"

"I dunno. I didn't think you were a joiner."

"I'm not," she admitted with a sigh. "But my mom thinks I'll never get into a good college if I don't do things outside of school."

He took the sheet from her. "You could join the gaming club. You like video games."

"Yeah, but somehow I don't think Mom will think that counts for college," Hannah said dryly.

"What about debate?"

"Me? I don't like to argue."

"You could use debate skills to convince your mom you don't need to join a club."

"I guess that's true." Hannah laughed. "But you know my mom—she would still win!"

"Good point." He handed the list back to her. "I don't know. I like doing stuff, but not when it's organized and has a grown-up in charge."

"Exactly," she said. "But we can't put that on a college application." She looked out the window at the snowy streets. "I wish Alexis hadn't gotten into Bailey. Then maybe Mom would be OK with me going to the U."

"How is Alexis anyway?" Jacob asked. "She took that breakup pretty hard."

"She's better." She turned to face him. "She has a new boyfriend I think. But they've never met in person."

Jacob raised his eyebrows. "Interesting. How did they meet? I mean, I'm sure it was online, but do you know what site or app?"

"Uh, good question. I have no idea."

/////

When Hannah got home she sat in the living room. Alexis wasn't home yet, and Hannah wondered if she was meeting that guy "IRL," as he had put it. But she came in about an hour later, looking at her phone and tapping on the screen as always.

"What's up?" Hannah called from the living room.

"Nothing. What's up with you?"

"Not much." Hannah waved the list of activities. "Want to help me pick an activity to get Mom off my back?"

Alexis sat down next to her but didn't take the list.

"Well, what do you *want* to do?" Alexis asked, sounding slightly annoyed.

"Nothing, but Mom thinks I should. For college."

"It won't help if you sign up for something just to put it on your college applications," Alexis said. "Believe me, lots of people do that."

"What's the point then?" Hannah tossed the list on the coffee table.

"Find something you're actually interested in," Alexis said. "And if that club doesn't exist, start it. That's what I did."

"Maybe I'll start a club for watching funny videos on the Internet."

"Ha. Good luck with that." Alexis rolled her eyes. She got up and started for the stairs, but stopped and turned back.

"If it makes you feel better, at least you're enjoying being a teenager more than I did."

"Really?" asked Hannah.

"Seriously. You hang out with friends and do fun stuff. I think you should put that on a college app: 'I know how to live.' That should count for something."

"Thanks, Alexis. But Mom won't buy it."

"I know," Alexis said. She came back into the room. "Can I tell you a secret?"

"Sure." *Maybe she's finally going to tell me about her virtual boyfriend*, Hannah thought.

Alexis sat down next to her. She took a deep breath and exhaled, then spoke quickly.

"I might not go to college next year."

Hannah's jaw dropped.

"But . . . but . . ." She stammered. "You've worked so hard to get into college. Not just any college—Bailey! It's one of the best schools in the country."

"Sometimes high school grads take a year off before college." Alexis swirled a lock of her hair around one finger, a habit she had when she was nervous. "It's called a gap year."

"I've heard of it," Hannah said. "But why you? Why now?"

"I know it seems out of the blue," said Alexis. "I've been thinking about it a lot, but I've been afraid to talk about it with our family.

I have talked to Eric—I mean *friends*," she quickly corrected herself.

So his name is Eric, Hannah thought. *I wonder how much he figures into this.*

"But that still doesn't explain why you're doing it," she said.

"I just feel like I'll need to catch my breath after high school before I jump back into things," Alexis said. She was still doing that thing with her hair. "The summer isn't enough."

"OK. I get that. But what about your scholarship?"

"Bailey will let me defer one year and still get the scholarship. The man I talked to even said they encourage it. He said students tend to do better if they wait a year."

"Wow," said Hannah—it was all she could say. "You've already talked to the Bailey people about it. That means you're serious about this."

"One hundred percent serious," Alexis said. "But don't tell Mom. Don't tell *anyone*."

"I won't, I swear," said Hannah.

"It feels good to tell someone," said Alexis.

"Practice for when I tell Mom." She stood up, glanced at her phone, and headed up to her room.

CHAPTER 2

After dinner, Hannah got on her main social media account and went to her sister's profile. She checked the relationship status. It still said "It's complicated." It had said that since she broke up with Chris. She browsed through her sister's friends, looking for guys named Eric. There were a couple, but not the guy she'd seen on Alexis's phone.

She wished there was some other way to learn more about this guy.

/////

"Find anything yet?" Jacob asked the next afternoon on the bus.

"Huh?" *Does he know I was trying to find out more about my sister's secret boyfriend?*

"To do outside of school," he added.

"Oh, yeah. I mean, no. Not yet. I was distracted." Hannah told him about Alexis's big news.

"That doesn't sound like Alexis," Jacob said. "I thought she had her whole life planned out so she'd be in charge of a big company before she turned thirty."

"She did!" said Hannah. "She does, I mean! But now it includes a gap year. So I guess she'll have to wait until she's thirty-one."

"How did your mom take it?"

"She doesn't know yet." Hannah clapped her hand over her mouth. "And I wasn't supposed to tell anyone," she admitted.

"Don't worry," he said. "It's not like *I'll* tell your mom."

"Still, don't say anything."

"My lips are sealed," he said. "Anyway, it's not a bad idea. Taking a year off just to chill. I think I'll do that too."

Hannah laughed. That was no surprise— Jacob wasn't really into school.

"Hey, do your parents give you a hard time?" She asked. "You don't belong to any clubs."

"I volunteer at an animal shelter," he said. "I walk the dogs. Play with the puppies. Stuff like that."

"Oh, yeah. I forgot." Jacob loved dogs, but he didn't have one.

"I even teach kids how to care for dogs," he said. "I went through a special training class to do it. Seeing those kids with their new pups . . . it's awesome."

"OK, OK. You do stuff." *And it'll look great on college applications*, Hannah guessed. *Especially if he goes to vet school or something.*

"So maybe you can volunteer somewhere," he suggested.

"That's a great idea," she said. "But I have to figure out where. I'm allergic to animals, and I don't know anything I can teach kids." She glanced out the window at a brick building: Mason Falls Senior Center. *But maybe it doesn't have to be kids.*

/////

Hannah tapped on her sister's door on Thursday. Alexis didn't come to the door, but Hannah could hear her voice through it. She was talking to somebody on the phone. Hannah tapped again, and Alexis pushed the door open.

"What's up? Having trouble with Wi-Fi?" The Wi-Fi worked better in Alexis's room, so sometimes Hannah worked in there.

"Not this time. I want to talk."

"Since when?" said Alexis, surprised.

"Since . . . since you told me your news," Hannah said in a quiet voice.

"Oh." Alexis let her in. "You're not going to tell Mom, are you?"

"No! I'm flattered you told *me*."

"I think I was practicing to tell Mom," said Alexis. She was holding her phone, but it was in sleep mode. *Was she talking to that guy just now?* Hannah wondered.

"She's going to find out sooner or later," she said.

"I know," said Alexis. "I'll tell her at the right time. Anyway, I made it official. I filled out a thing online. It was super easy."

"Wow. What will you do all year?"

"Oh, get a part-time job," Alexis said. "Save up spending money for college. My scholarship covers my expenses but doesn't give me anything extra. And mostly I'll try to enjoy being a teenager while I still can."

"That sounds good," said Hannah, trying to sound supportive. *But it doesn't sound like Alexis*, she thought.

"What's up with you?" Alexis asked. "Did you find something to do to get Mom off your back?"

"Yes! I'm going to help people at the senior center with computer stuff. Sending emails, video chatting with their families, those kinds of things. I went over there after school to suggest it. They said they'd been trying to find someone to do that for months."

"Hannah, that's awesome!"

"Thanks." Hannah felt her face get hot. Alexis rarely complimented her, but maybe she was trying to thank her for keeping her secret. Hannah had devised a plan, though, and Alexis's new friendliness would help.

"Hey, do you want to watch movies this weekend? Mom and Wayne are going out tomorrow, so I thought we could have a sisters' night. You can pick the movies."

Alexis looked surprised. "Really? Like hang out together?"

"Why not? Sometimes sisters do that."

"I know, it's just been a long time since we have," said Alexis. "But sure, I'd like that. I had plans that kind of fell through, so sure." She peeked back at her computer. "But right now I'm in the middle of something so . . ."

"No problem. I can go." Hannah headed for the door.

"Seriously, congrats on the volunteer gig," Alexis said as she was shutting the door behind her.

/////

When Hannah's mom dropped her off at the senior center on Saturday morning, she was worried that nobody would want her help. But there was already a line of six people. She felt a knot in her stomach.

They do know I'm just a high school sophomore, right? Hannah worried.

But her nervousness soon faded. She helped Elmer rotate some photos that were sideways. She helped Susan search through a genealogy website. She helped Charles filter his email so he wasn't drowning in spam. They were all easy problems to solve, and the seniors were really grateful.

I like this, she thought, *and not just for the sake of getting into a good college. I like doing it.*

The fourth person in line was Dorothy.

"I got an email from my bank, and it says my account has been hacked. But when I try to log in, I can't."

"Show me," Hannah said.

Dorothy opened her email and clicked on a message. It said Dorothy's account had been "compromised." It looked really official, but Hannah wasn't convinced.

"Did you call the bank?"

"No, I followed the link they gave me." She pointed at the bold, underlined link telling her to "verify your account now."

"Uh-oh." Hannah put her mouse on the link but didn't click. The URL appeared in a yellow pop-up. She could see the link was *not* going to the banking website.

"It's a fake," she said.

"But it has the bank name in the web address," said Dorothy. "And it looks exactly like the one I'm used to."

"But the web address ends in *dot to*, not *dot com*." Hannah pointed out the letters. "Easy to miss if you're in a hurry."

"Or if you have bad eyesight," said Dorothy. "They are so slick."

"Did you enter your password?"

"Well, yes. I thought I was verifying my account."

Hannah's heart sank.

"Call your bank right away," she said. "Tell them what happened so they freeze your account."

She waited while Dorothy called. She felt as nervous as if her own grandmother had been tricked by a scam artist.

Dorothy talked for a while, explaining the

situation, and then covered the mouthpiece to give Hannah an update.

"Somebody did log in to my account, but the bank blocked it because it was from another country."

"Whew," Hannah said.

Dorothy changed her password over the phone. After hanging up, she beamed at Hannah.

"We fixed it."

"What a relief," said Hannah.

"I'm so glad I could talk to you instead of my son," said Dorothy. "He always makes me feel so stupid. You don't." She patted her hand. "I'm no dummy. But you know, these scammers are really clever. Being smart isn't enough to be safe anymore."

"I know," Hannah agreed. She thought about Alexis and her online boyfriend. *What if Eric isn't who he says he is? What if he's some kind of scam artist?*

Alexis was smart, but like Dorothy said, being smart wasn't enough.

CHAPTER 3

Alexis wasn't home when Hannah got there.

What if she's meeting Eric right now? If that's even his real name . . .

But Alexis sent her a text an hour later.

Still on for movies?

Yes! Hannah wrote back. *Where are you?*

Planning a fundraiser for my Future Women Leaders group.

Hannah sighed with relief. *Of course that's where she is*, she thought. That was exactly the kind of thing Alexis was usually up to. And it meant she hadn't completely changed, even with Eric in her life and with her plan to take a gap year.

Later that afternoon, Hannah heated oil in the kettle, poured in some popcorn, and put on the lid. Alexis got home as it was popping, the delicious smell wafting through the house. Hannah had planned it that way.

"Want some?" she asked.

"Of course. You know it's my favorite. But not too much butter!" Alexis took off her coat and hung it by the door. "Time to change into sweats. Meet you in the living room?"

"You bet."

Hannah tossed the popcorn in a big bowl with melted butter. Lots and lots of melted butter. That was part of her plan.

She peered into the living room and saw Alexis was back, flipping through the streaming movie options. Hannah waited until Alexis's phone buzzed.

That's my cue!

Hannah grabbed the popcorn bowl and hurried out. She stumbled and sent half the bowl raining down over the back of the couch and down Alexis's front. Her sister jumped up, leaving her phone on the coffee table.

"Sorry!" Hannah said. "I tripped over my own feet." Alexis started to reach for her phone but saw that her hands were greasy with butter from the popcorn. "Ugh!" She dashed into the kitchen to wash her hands.

"So sorry!" Hannah said. She picked up her sister's phone. Sure enough, Eric was texting her again. His last message was open.

See you then. <3

Hannah rolled her eyes. He was signing off with sideways hearts! She tapped on his name to get his profile, took a screenshot, and attached the image to a new message. She started to send it to herself but stopped. She'd left her phone in the kitchen. What if Alexis heard the beep and glanced at it? She would see that the message was coming from her own phone! Hannah typed in Jacob's number instead.

He already knows about the online boyfriend. It won't be hard to explain this, Hannah thought.

It's Hannah, reply to my real number, she typed out. The water turned off in the kitchen, so she only had a few seconds. She sent the message, deleted it from Alexis's sent messages, and deleted the screenshot from her photos folder. She put the phone down a split second before Alexis came back in.

"Sorry," she said again. She raked kernels of popcorn from the couch cushions onto the floor.

"Accidents happen," said Alexis. "Hey, is there still enough to eat?"

"Plenty. But first I have to vacuum."

When she was in the hall, she heard her own phone beeping from the kitchen. She ran in and grabbed it. There was a message from Jacob.

Why are you sending me some guy's profile?

Hannah peeked at Alexis. She was on her phone, typing out a message with one hand and eating popcorn with the other. She was paying no attention to Hannah.

It's Alexis's Internet boyfriend, Hannah typed back. *Send it to me.*

Jacob forwarded the screenshot to her, followed by a shrugging-guy emoji.

"I found a movie I want to see!" Alexis called.

"Be right there!" Hannah sent a quick *TTYL* and shoved the phone in her pocket.

/////

They watched a movie and ate popcorn. Alexis even mostly stayed off her phone.

"Thanks," Alexis said when the movie was over. "That was nice and sisterly."

"Ha. No problem." Hannah felt a pang of guilt that the whole thing was a setup.

In her room, she transferred the screenshot to her computer and cropped the picture of Eric. It was a bit corny—dashing smile, shiny hair. The kind of photo that some kids had for the yearbook. But he was a good-looking guy, no doubt about it. She ran a reverse-image search. Only one match turned up, and it was on a social media site she'd never heard of. "The only social site exclusively for ages eighteen to twenty-one," it advertised. After clicking around, Hannah realized it was a dating site. Was this where Alexis had met him?

The profile was for Eric, a "serious guy with a sense of humor." He wanted to go into business and work for himself someday. So did Alexis. He liked movies, especially comedies, and didn't care about sports. Same as Alexis. His list of top five bands could have been Alexis's own top five list. *I can see why she would respond to him*, she thought. *But is it too perfect?* She thought about how well the scammers had faked Dorothy's banking website. Maybe somebody mocked up the perfect match for Alexis.

Who are you really, Eric?

She browsed a dozen different websites that offered reverse searches for phone numbers. There were free searches, but they only worked for landlines. Any that searched for cell phones cost a few dollars. The websites looked fishy to her. And if she used one, she would have to use her debit card, which meant her mom would see she'd spent money on a shady website. She was thinking about doing it anyway when Alexis burst in.

"Why did you use my phone?" she demanded.

"Huh?" Hannah looked at her sister. "I didn't."

"I can see you sent a message to someone."

She held up her phone. It was open to the message app. There was a "Recent" label followed by a few names. Jacob's number was at the top, just above Eric. "I don't know whose number that is. And you're the only one who could have used my phone besides me."

Oops. Hannah had thought deleting the text would be enough to cover her trail.

"I didn't mean to use your phone," she sputtered. "I didn't even know I did."

"Sure you didn't." Alexis was fuming.

"We do have the same model phone," Hannah said. "I honestly don't remember messaging Jacob." She snapped her fingers and pretended to look like she just remembered something. "Just before the movie. I must have grabbed your phone off the coffee table and sent off a message by mistake."

"I don't remember that."

"You were out of the room, washing your hands from the popcorn."

"Uh, hi girls," said a voice. Wayne, their stepdad, was at the top of the stairs. He and their mom had gotten home.

"Oh, hi." Hannah moved out of the way. Wayne nodded at them and hurried into the master bedroom. He never meddled in their business.

"I looked in my sent messages and there wasn't anything from this evening," Alexis whispered fiercely.

"So what's the big deal?" asked Hannah.

"There should be one," Alexis said. "If this guy's in the recent folder, somebody messaged him from my phone. And if it was an accident, the message wouldn't be deleted."

Hannah didn't know what to say. She was busted.

"Maybe I should check the trash," said Alexis. "Did you remember to empty the trash?"

"Um." Hannah knew she was sunk. She should have thought about the trash.

Alexis was tapping on the phone. In a moment, she would see the message with the attached screenshot.

"I wanted to know more about this guy you're texting," she blurted. "Because . . .

because . . ." She remembered that Wayne was thirty feet away. "Because I was curious."

"Ha!" said Alexis. "I knew it. So what did you send to Jacob and why?"

"Eric's profile picture. Because . . . oh, forget it."

"No, I won't forget it. You sneaky little traitor!"

"What's going on?" their mom asked, coming up the stairs.

"Hannah was snooping on my phone. Reading my *private* messages."

"Just one message," Hannah protested.

"And sharing them with her friends!" Alexis added.

"It wasn't even a message. It was a photo."

"Hannah," their mom said. "Respect your sister's privacy."

If you only knew what this was about, thought Hannah. But she bit her tongue.

"Sorry," she said. She gave her sister a look. *Be glad I haven't told Mom about your gap year*, she thought. *Not to mention your online boyfriend.*

"Why don't you get your own life instead of meddling in mine?" Alexis said.

"Alexis!" said their mom. "You have a right to be mad, but that wasn't necessary. Say you're sorry."

"I'm sorry you don't have a life," Alexis said. She went back to her room and slammed the door.

CHAPTER 4

Alexis barely spoke to her all week. Not even a grunt if Hannah asked her to pass the cereal. She drove Hannah to school, as always, but the rides went by in silence.

The girls spent the following weekend with their dad. He used to plan things for their visits, like trips to the zoo or the museum, but when they became teenagers he stopped trying to make the weekends fun. So the girls couldn't help being bored, cooped up in a condo thirty miles from all their friends. Alexis spent the weekend sitting on the floor in the room they shared, her phone plugged into the wall. Hannah did homework, finishing the novel for

English class and doing a history timeline that wasn't due for two weeks. By Sunday night, she had worked as far ahead as she could and wished Monday wasn't a holiday.

"What do you want to do tomorrow?" their dad asked. "I don't have to work, and I don't want to spend another day sitting around watching you two glare at each other."

"I'm not glaring," Hannah protested.

"Just peeking and prying," Alexis muttered.

"Enough!" their dad said. "I miss the weekends where we would make teddy bears or drive out to the biggest candy store in the state."

"Me too," said Hannah. She gave Alexis a look.

"Then take Hannah to make a teddy bear and get candy," said Alexis.

"Not that," their dad said. "Let's do something girls your age do."

"You mean women," said Alexis. "I'm eighteen."

"Right," their dad said. "Look, the two of you can choose. Maybe it'll be good for you to have to talk to each other."

"I want to stay here," Alexis said between clenched teeth.

"I want to go somewhere with no cell phone service," Hannah said.

"Maybe I'll go bowling and leave you two alone," their dad complained.

They actually *did* go bowling, but they played three rounds without exchanging more than a few words. They ate fried fish sandwiches at a nearby restaurant, then their dad took them home. Hannah could tell he couldn't wait to be rid of both of them. The girls had never been best friends, but usually they could get along for a few hours.

"I'm really sorry I looked at your phone," she told Alexis on the drive back. "Can you please let it go?"

"Sure," Alexis said, but she clearly didn't mean it. "Whatever."

/////

On Thursday the girls still weren't talking, and Alexis didn't come home after school.

Hannah paced in the upstairs hallway. Her sister had been home *last* Thursday after school, which meant she didn't have a club that met on this day. Of course, she could be at the library, or out with friends . . .

Alexis had left her bedroom door open. Hannah peered into the room. It was already getting dark outside. A shadowy mound on the bed caught her eye.

She pushed the door open a bit wider and let in the light from the hallway. Sweaters, blouses, and jeans were strewn all over the room. It looked like Alexis had tried on everything she owned that morning. As if she'd been really worried about how she looked. As if she was meeting a special person for the first time.

She's probably meeting Eric, she thought. *Right now.*

Hannah heard the door open downstairs. She quickly walked back to her own room and lay on the bed, grabbing her history textbook off the desk.

Alexis came up the stairs. She started for her own room, then walked into Hannah's. She looked really sad.

"Hey, Han," she said mildly.

"Hi." She was glad Alexis was talking to her, but acted like it was no big deal.

"What are you reading about?" her sister asked.

"The Great Depression." Hannah peered up over the book. "Everything OK?"

"Fine. Fine." Alexis dropped her smile. "I got stood up."

"What?" Hannah set her book down. "Who? Why?"

"Eric. We were supposed to have coffee, but he didn't show. He sent a text half an hour late. He said he had car trouble."

"Well, maybe he really did have car trouble," said Hannah. "It *is* cold outside."

"Maybe, but he's done it before," she said. "Every time we try to meet in person, he has car trouble, or he gets sick, or something else comes up."

"Wait," Hannah jolted up in bed, trying to look shocked. "You've never met him in person?"

"He lives really far away," Alexis explained. "In Silver Valley. He's a freshman at the U. It's a four hour drive . . . Don't look at me like that! He's less than one year older than me."

"How do you know him at all if you haven't met in person?" asked Hannah.

"I was bored one night and feeling lonely so I went to this dating site. I thought I was just goofing around, but Eric was so much like me I sent him a message. He's into the same things. Really sweet and funny."

"He sounds nice."

"It would be great if he could ever get it together and meet me in person," said Alexis. "I don't want to marry an avatar."

"Wait, what? *Marry?*" Hannah said in shock.

"You know what I mean," Alexis said quickly.

Hannah felt queasy—the sister she knew was always careful with her words. *What if Alexis is really thinking about marrying this guy?*

"But hey, thanks for listening," said Alexis. "And don't tell Mom about this. Or anyone."

"I won't."

"And thanks for not telling them about the, uh, the gap year."

"Of course." *Now I have two big secrets to keep for Alexis*, Hannah thought.

Alexis drifted back to her room. Hannah tried to study for real, but was too distracted.

She heard her mom come in, and a few minutes later the doorbell rang. She heard her mom talking to someone, then yelling up the stairs.

"Alexis! It's for you!"

Hannah felt a jolt of surprise. *He's here*, she thought. She fought the urge to run down and see if she was right. But Eric didn't know where Alexis lived—did he?

She heard Alexis going down the stairs and talking to their mom. Hannah crept to the top of the stairs and looked down. Alexis was holding a bouquet of flowers. Their mom was reading the card.

"'Sorry about today. Hope our plans haven't changed.' What does that mean?" their mom asked. "Who sent these?"

"Chris," Alexis said automatically. "We had a fight today."

"I thought you broke up."

"We did," she said. "But back when we broke up, we agreed that if neither of us was dating someone else by prom, we'd go together as friends, so we wouldn't have to go alone. Well, he still wants to go and I said it was too soon to talk about it. That's why we argued. And that's what he means about the plans."

"Oh," said Mom. She handed the card back.

"Not that it's any of your business," said Alexis, snatching it back.

"I'm your mother. It *is* my business," she said. "But I am sorry he's making this hard."

"Boys," Alexis said with a shrug.

"I can put the flowers on the dining room table," their mom offered.

"Nah, I'll take them up to my room." Alexis started up the stairs. When their mom stepped back into the kitchen, Alexis dipped her face into the flowers and took a deep, happy breath. She looked blissful. She looked like she was in love.

Hannah hurried back to her own room before Alexis saw her.

She's lying to Mom, Hanna thought. *The flowers must be from Eric. Which means he does know where we live.*

/////

Later that night Hannah reverse-searched the image of Eric again. She's already tried it, but she didn't have any other ideas. Now the search didn't work at all. He must have taken down his profile. That could be a good sign. *Hopefully he shut it down because he's serious about Alexis.*

"Are you looking for polo shirts?" the search engine asked, which was both weirdly correct—Eric was wearing one—and way off. Hannah clicked on "related images," and saw a grid of smiling, clean-cut guys in short-sleeved collared shirts. Definitely Alexis's type, but not hers.

She scrolled down, laughing to herself at the sameness of them all. She noticed one and clicked on it.

It was Eric. It was the same guy, wearing a similar shirt but from a different angle. The image was from an online clothing store.

Hannah found that she could change his shirt color with a click. So she did, trading in the deep green for the shirt that he was wearing in the picture Alexis had. A sick feeling bubbled in her stomach.

The shirt was from the Three Seasons collection. She clicked into a page for that collection. The home page showed four guys, all wearing different shirts, trying to look natural. Eric was one of them and looked exactly the same as his profile picture. The image search hadn't found this because in his profile, he'd used only a small part of the whole photo. Maybe he'd done that on purpose, knowing people might reverse-search the image.

In any case, unless Eric was a male model, he was using a fake photo.

CHAPTER 5

Hannah dropped into the seat next to Jacob on the bus ride home the next day.

"Hi!" she said with a grin.

"Uh, hi." He narrowed his eyes. "You're going to ask me for something, aren't you?"

Hannah tried to grin a little less broadly. "Can I borrow your debit card?"

"Uh . . . no?"

"I'll pay you for the charge," she said. "And it's only a few bucks." He shook his head. "I would use my own, but my mother reads the statement," she went on. "And you told me once that your mom doesn't notice what you use yours for."

"She might. If it's something weird and expensive."

"This is a little weird but not expensive."

He sighed. "What are you up to, Hannah?"

Hannah told him about using a website to reverse search Eric's phone number. "Those websites all say, like, 'cell phone user found,' but you have to pay to actually see the name."

"Good grief," he said. "Have you tried *asking your sister* about this guy?"

"Well, yeah," Hannah said. "But Alexis only knows what he's told her, and now I know he's a liar. I already figured out he's using a fake photo."

"Lots of guys probably use fake photos."

"Maybe. But if he's lying about that, he could be lying about . . . well, everything. Maybe the next time his car breaks down, he'll ask Alexis for her debit card number for repairs. Or, I know." She snapped her fingers. "His car breaks down on the way, and he's stranded. She sends him her card info for a motel room and a meal. I've seen stories about stuff like that happening. But of course there is no car or motel room. There isn't even a guy in Silver Valley. It's some guy in, like, a sketchy apartment somewhere, and he cleans out her bank account."

"I've heard stories like that too," Jacob said slowly. "But I don't want to enter my debit card number into some website."

"They are a little sketchy," she admitted. "But I don't know what else to do. This is serious, Jacob."

"I get that," he said.

"He already knows where we live," Hannah added. "I'm pretty sure he sent Alexis flowers."

"Criminals in sketchy apartments probably wouldn't send flowers," he said.

"Who knows?" Hannah said.

The bus brakes hissed and the bus rolled to a stop.

"All right, come on," Jacob said. "This is where I get off."

"Really? You're going to help me?"

"Yeah, I'll help. Not sure how yet, but if you're worried . . . And Alexis is nice and I don't want her to be in any trouble. So let's go."

"Thanks, Jacob!"

She followed him down an icy sidewalk to the duplex where he lived. Hannah remembered crowding around Jacob's kitchen table with two others boys, playing games all weekend. Jacob's mom would make them pizza rolls and nachos.

"I miss our gaming sessions," she said.

"Me too," he said. "Anyway, I have an idea." He opened his backpack and took out his cheap laptop. "Do you know where that guy ordered the flowers?"

"Ugh. No."

"I thought maybe we could call the flower shop and find out who sent them."

"Good idea."

"So, flower shops." He entered a search. A list of flower shops in the area showed up. "Too many to try calling all of them," he said.

"Yeah," she agreed. She nudged him over and clicked on a couple. "Maybe we can find the exact bouquet he sent." She checked one website, then another, looking for the arrangement Alexis had gotten. She found the exact bouquet halfway down the list of florists. It was featured on the front page of one flower shop's website. It even had the same green vase her sister's had come in. "Spring Love," it was called. Black-eyed Susans and baby's breath.

"This is it," she said. "But what if they don't tell us who sent it?"

"It's worth a shot," Jacob said.

"You're right." Hannah called the number and a cheerful woman answered. Hannah stammered through an explanation. She wanted to thank someone for the lovely flowers she'd received, but they'd arrived anonymously.

"Often our senders do want to maintain an air of mystery and romance," the woman said.

"Yeah, but can you tell me who they're from?"

"Sorry," the woman said. "We don't disclose that information out of respect for our customers' privacy."

"Thanks anyway," Hannah said and hung up. "Dead end. Want to try that reverse search?"

Jacob sighed. "OK, find the least shady looking site that does reverse searches. Meanwhile I'm gonna grab a snack."

While Jacob rummaged around on the kitchen counter, Hannah found a blog where someone had reviewed several of the phone search websites. She went to the one they recommended most. "Cheap and no shenanigans," the review said.

"Hey, this one is only a dollar," she said as Jacob rejoined her with a bag of pretzels.

"That's good," Jacob said. He handed her his card and she entered the numbers.

A few second later they got a report: E ROGERS, at an address in a town twenty miles away. She took a snapshot of the address with her phone.

"All that for a first initial and a last name," Jacob said.

"It's something," she said. "The first initial is E. That's a good sign, right?"

"True," Jacob said. "You owe me a dollar."

/////

Hannah walked home, slipping a little on the icy sidewalks. As soon as she got to her room, she started searching the web for Eric Rogers.

She started with the university where Eric supposedly was a freshman. There were three students at the U named Eric Rogers. No, two. One *Erica* had shown up in the search results.

Hannah took a closer look. One of the Erics had the word *Faculty* under "type." The other type was *Graduate*. Eric was supposedly a freshman. So neither of these people named Eric Rogers could be her sister's boyfriend, unless he lied about his age, which would be super creepy.

Hannah drummed her fingers on the desktop. Students could probably be unlisted if they wanted to. But how likely was that? How many eighteen and nineteen-year-old men needed to go into hiding? It seemed more likely that Alexis's Eric was lying about going to the U. Or she didn't have the right name. The reverse search could have out-of-date info, and the E could be a coincidence.

She searched a few social media sites, but Eric Rogers was a popular name. Thousands of guys were walking around with that name, and she didn't have any luck filtering by college or hometown. How else could you track down someone? What did private detectives do? She imagined herself lying low in a car, watching a house and waiting for someone to leave, like detectives did in movies.

Someone tapped on her door. She closed her laptop.

"Come in!"

"Hey, it's me." Alexis crept in and closed the door behind her. She was trembling.

"What's wrong? Are you all right?"

"I don't know," she said. She dropped to the bed. She fanned herself with her hand even though it was cold in the room.

"Alexis?"

"Han," her sister said. "I'm going to tell you something and you can't tell *anyone*. And you can't freak out."

"Uh . . . OK? I mean, I'll try. But if you think I *might*, then I might do it anyway."

Alexis took in a deep breath and let it out.

"You know Eric?"

"Yes," she said slowly. *This can't be good*, she thought. "I mean, I obviously don't know him, but . . . you get it."

"Well, OK," Alexis said. "One of the reasons I thought about a gap year is, well, because I wanted to see where this went, and he lives near here, but Bailey is like a thousand miles away. And then he stood me up three times, and I thought, maybe this is silly. And I was ready to call it off."

Did she break up with him? Hannah wondered. *Can I quit being Sherlock Hannah because Alexis finally realized this is ridiculous?*

"By the way, those flowers really were from him," Alexis went on. "And I really appreciated them, but I thought about it and I told him, you know, if you're afraid to even meet, maybe we should just call this off, and *he* said . . ."

"He said OK?" Hannah guessed.

"He said, 'I'll show you I'm not afraid,'" Alexis said. "And he proposed."

CHAPTER 6

Hannah wanted to yell, but she kept her voice steady.

"He proposed via text?" she asked. "That's not very . . . romantic."

"It wasn't by text, it was over the phone. And he said I'll get a proper proposal. Bended knee and everything. But he wanted me to know he was serious about *me*, Han."

"What did you say?"

"I said when he asked me for real, in person, I would have an answer."

"But you wouldn't put him through it unless you were going to say yes, right?"

Alexis got a dreamy look on her face.

"Wow." Hannah felt cold. None of this felt real. Alexis had planned her whole life out, gotten into Bailey. And now she was basically engaged to some dude she hadn't even met yet? But if Hannah argued with Alexis now, Alexis might shut Hannah out again, as she had for almost a week. And if she did that, Hannah wouldn't get any more information from her. Like when and where she and Eric would meet.

"When is this going to happen?"

"Well, after I graduate from high school, obviously. Maybe we'll just—elope, you know? Instead of waiting around for Mom to go nuts. I mean, we'd talked about both taking the year off and going somewhere together. Some place with a beach and lots of jobs. Florida, maybe. So we'd still do that, only now . . . now we would be husband and wife." She got the dreamy look again.

"I mean, when will he propose?" Hannah said. Even if Eric was exactly who he said he was, this was scary stuff—Alexis couldn't get married to a guy she'd never met in person.

"Saturday. He's getting his car back tomorrow, so he can drive up to meet me."

"Wow," Hannah said. Saturday—so soon.

"I know it's hard to understand," Alexis said. "But if you knew Eric, you would get it. If you could hear us talk, how we finish each other's sentences and read each other's minds . . . We're so perfect for each other. I can feel it even when we're not together."

"You do seem really happy," said Hannah. She got up and hugged her sister. *Act like you're happy for her or she'll stop talking to you.*

"I want you to be my maid of honor," Alexis whispered.

"Of course," Hannah whispered back.

And then Alexis flew out of the room, back to her phone and her virtual fiancé.

This has gone too far. I have to do something, Hannah thought.

/////

On Saturday morning, Hannah volunteered at the senior center again, helping a dozen retired folks download attachments, update their browsers, and reset their passwords. There was nothing serious this time, like Dorothy's hacked bank account, but there was a steady stream of people wanting advice. At the back of her mind, Hannah kept thinking about Alexis. Eric was supposed to come to town *today*. They'd go out tonight and he'd propose. It was hard to believe.

A couple of the seniors handed her five-dollar bills as tips for her time. At first, Hannah refused, but they were insistent.

"Do you know what computer professionals charge?" one woman asked her in a low voice. "And they don't explain things half as well as you. Take it. I have plenty of money."

So Hannah had some spending money, and it was lunchtime, and she was hungry. There was a café in the strip mall across the street. She headed over and ordered some food.

As she waited for her sandwich, she sent a text to Alexis.

So is it on? What's up?

Her sister didn't respond. Maybe the proposal plans were called off and she didn't want to talk about it? Hannah could only hope.

After she'd finished eating, Hannah stepped outside and noticed a flower shop at the other end of the strip mall. It was the same chain that Eric Rogers had used.

She figured all the stores were connected by computer. She could step in and ask who'd sent those flowers to Alexis. Maybe if she asked in person, someone would be more likely to help. She would tell them some guy was pestering her. Nothing that required police action, but he needed to knock it off.

Hannah had a story all ready when she walked in, but there was nobody at the counter. A sign said "ring for service," and next to it was a bell. Whoever worked here must be taking a break.

Hannah noticed a handset to a cordless phone also sitting on the counter. She had an idea. A call from the phone would show up as the flower shop on someone's caller ID. It was too good an opportunity to pass up. She plucked up the phone and carried it to the corner. She pulled out her own phone to look at the screenshot she'd taken at Jacob's house. It showed Eric's phone number and—supposedly—his address. She tapped out his number on the cordless phone.

"Hello?" a guy answered.

Hannah made her own voice raspy to sound older. "This is Emily calling from the flower shop," she said. "You ordered flowers two days ago? The spring love bouquet, delivered to 2675 Sunset Drive?"

"Yeah," he said. "That was only half the order, but it was me. What's wrong?"

Only half the order? Is he romancing two different girls? Never mind. Get his name.

"We had a problem processing your credit card," Hannah said. "Can you just confirm the name on the card?"

"You need the number again?"

"Just the name, sir."

"Uh, sure," he said. "It's Pat Derringer." Just then, the clerk came in. She saw Hannah with the phone and looked puzzled.

"Ah, thank you, have a good day." Hannah hit the big red button, cutting off Eric. Or rather, Patrick.

"Are you using our phone?" the clerk asked. She sounded more surprised than upset.

"Sorry." She handed the woman the phone. "I needed to make an urgent call. It was local." She hurried out before the woman could say anything else. Then she took out her own phone and dialed Jacob's number as she walked across the strip mall parking lot. He answered on the fourth ring.

"Hey. Since when do you *call*? You usually just text."

"It's an emergency." Hannah stopped by a bench at the edge of the parking lot and sat down. "Alexis's boyfriend isn't who he says he is."

"How do you know?"

"I called him." Hannah explained how she'd made the call from the flower shop.

"Wow. Tricked him with the caller ID," Jacob said. "Smart move."

"Exactly."

"So what's his real name?" Jacob asked.

"Pat Derringer. Or maybe Pat Berringer. I didn't have time to ask him to spell it." That clerk had walked in while she was talking to him. "In any case, it isn't Eric. Let's just call him Fakey McLiesalot."

"So, uh. I hate to be . . . Poppy McBubbleburst," Jacob said, playing on her own words. "But you asked for the name on the *credit card*."

"So?" Hannah already saw her mistake, but didn't want to admit it.

"So maybe it wasn't his own card," Jacob said. "Maybe his mom reads his credit card reports so he went to a gullible friend."

"Oh, come on! Jacob!"

"I'm sort of kidding," he said. "But it could be his dad's card. Or even his mom's."

"The name on it was Patrick," she said.

"You said Pat before. It could be short for Patricia."

"Ugh, you're right. But anyway, it's a lead," she insisted. "A much better one than we had before. Can you do some more web searches? I think you might need to spend another dollar or two to get all the info on someone. Find addresses for anyone named Pat Derringer. Either in Silver Valley or closer to Mason Falls."

"Uh, sure," he said. "Right now?"

"If you can. I was hoping you could get his info while I go home and see what Alexis is doing."

"OK. Fine. I'll try to find this Pat Dillinger."

"Derringer," she corrected.

"Patrick or Patricia Derringer," he echoed. "I'll see what I can do."

CHAPTER 7

Hannah hurried home, hoping to find Alexis sitting on the couch flipping through TV channels or at least up in her room. Instead, she found her mother at the dining room table, looking through cookbooks and jotting down a grocery list.

"Is Alexis here?" Hannah asked, trying to sound casual.

"No," her mother said. "How was the senior center?"

"Fine. Do you know where she is?"

"No idea," her mom said casually.

"Seriously?" Her mother usually kept close tabs on her daughters.

"She's eighteen," her mother reminded her. "A responsible adult, remember?"

"I know."

"She's going to move out in six months. I have to get used to it. Maybe letting her disappear on Saturday afternoons is a good start."

"I guess," Hannah agreed. She started for the stairs.

"Wait," her mother said before she was two steps up. "Since you mentioned Alexis, there's something I want to talk about."

From the way her mom was pushing the cookbooks and list aside, it would be a serious talk. For a moment, Hannah wondered if her mom had guessed part of what was going on with Alexis. But she'd just said she wasn't worried about her older daughter, so that couldn't be what this was about.

Hannah's phone buzzed. She glanced at it and saw a notification: *Jacob: [image]*. She couldn't see the photo he'd sent while her screen was locked.

"Put your phone away," her mother said, pulling out a chair. "Let's talk."

Her mother was still worried about her fight with Alexis from the week before. "Tell me what's going on with you two. You really can tell me anything."

Hannah felt like she was on a tight rope, trying to tell her mother what the fight was about without mentioning Eric or the gap year. Somehow, she managed.

Her phone buzzed constantly while she and her mother talked.

It was nearly two o'clock by the time Hannah finally got up to her room and managed to check her messages. The image from Jacob was a screen shot of a search for Patricia Derringer. It was followed by several texts from Jacob.

Looks like I was right. Pat is E's mom. Same address as E. Rogers.

Not too far from here.

So I guess that mystery is solved.

Well?

Message me back!

Hannah started to but first messaged Alexis.

Where are you?

She was beginning to worry. What if Alexis was meeting Eric right now? What if he had been on his way to meet her when Hannah had called him? It hadn't sounded like he was in his car, but who knew? Alexis hadn't said when exactly Eric was supposed to show up. Hannah didn't think anyone would pop the question on an afternoon date to a coffee shop, but nothing about Alexis's relationship was normal.

To Hannah's relief, a text came from Alexis right away. It was a photo of two blouses side by side on a dressing room bench. They were the same design, but one was turquoise, the other scarlet.

Which do you like better?

Hannah sighed relief. Her sister was shopping. Of course. She had a big date tonight.

You look better in blue, she texted back.

Thanks! I know E's favorite color is red, but blue it is.

Hannah sent back a smiling emoji. She felt more like gagging.

What next?

She knew Eric's address. If he wasn't really a student, he probably still lived with his mom, and it wasn't *that* far away.

She messaged Jacob.

Thanks for the info. Want to take a road trip?

Sure. Should we take your car or mine? He added a winking emoji because neither of them had a car.

You have a license, she reminded him. *Was hoping you could use your mom's car.*

She never lets me drive, he said.

Never ever? Hannah asked.

Almost never.

Tell her it's an emergency. Tell her you're helping a friend.

What kind of emergency?

Hannah scanned the room, looking for ideas. She saw her history timeline in the corner, the one that she'd done at her dad's house last weekend.

I need to get something from my dad's house. Tell her I left a homework project there and my mom can't take me.

Just a sec.

He messaged her again a few seconds later.

She says OK.

You're both awesome. Be right over.

She ran downstairs.

"I'm going to Jacob's," she told her mother.

"Really? Starting up that gaming group again?"

"No, we're doing a research project together." It wasn't even a lie.

"OK. Let me know if you won't be home for dinner."

"I will." She put on her coat and boots and started over, realizing as she walked that her phone battery was nearly drained. She hoped Jacob's mom had a charger in her car.

Jacob met her on the porch. They climbed into the car, and Hannah didn't see a charger. She'd have to go off the grid for a while.

"So are we going to Pat Berringer's house?" Jacob asked.

"Derringer," she said. "And yes."

"You're paying for gas, right?"

"Absolutely." Hannah was glad she still had cash from her customers at the senior center. Sometimes she bought Alexis gas, but their mom might ask if she saw a big charge on Hannah's debit card report. Jacob backed out of the driveway and drove slowly down the street.

"This is only like the third time she's let me drive alone," he said.

"You're doing fine."

After getting gas, they headed out of town.

"Put your dad's address into the GPS," he said. "Mom'll see it later and think that's where we went."

"Smart. It's like you've tricked your mom before."

"I said it's the third time she's let me drive the car. Not the first." Jacob grinned.

Hannah put in the address, mapped it, then turned off the guidance.

"So what'll we do when we get there?" Jacob asked.

"First, see if he's there. He's supposed to be going to the U, so if he's at home instead of in Silver Valley, it'll mean he lied about that."

"Unless he stopped in to see his mom on his way to meet Alexis."

"Maybe," she said. Jacob saw the flaws in all of her theories. "But I think we'll know if he's sketchy."

"Mmhmm," he agreed. "What's our cover story?"

"Good question." She would need to ask for Eric, but if he found out she was Alexis's sister, word would get back to Alexis. Maybe she would just have to risk it. "Let's play it by ear."

"Oh sure, the classic strategy."

"Well, do you have a better idea?" she shot back.

"Nope, I wasn't even being sarcastic. Winging it is my usual MO, so I'm fine with that."

"Thanks for doing this," she said. "You're a good friend."

"It's fine," he said. "It's kind of fun. A real-life mystery."

Once they reached Eric's hometown, Jacob used his phone to navigate. He pulled in front of a house with pale yellow siding.

"That must be it," he said. "At least there's no boards on the windows to block out the sunlight."

"I didn't think he was a *vampire*," Hannah said.

"Still a good sign," Jacob said.

They went up to the house and rang the bell. There was a long silence, then eyes at the window. A woman opened the door.

"Hello?"

"We're looking for Eric Rogers?" Hannah said.

"He's not home," she said. "Is this about his ad?"

"Um . . . yes," Hannah said. She had no idea what ad the woman was talking about, but figured it might get them in the door.

"Are you here about the bike or the video game?"

"The game," Hannah said.

The woman led them into the house. "I don't know why he suddenly decided to sell everything. True, he never rides his bike anymore, but if he finds a job he'll need it. And the video game. It cost a lot more than what he's selling it for, but I'm glad to be rid of it. It seems like all he does is play games."

So Eric was a big-time gamer. His profile hadn't said anything about that.

Hannah scanned the room. There was a china hutch with a vase of flowers. And some pictures, one of a boy who looked nothing like Eric's profile picture.

"Nice flowers," she said. It was the exact same arrangement he'd sent Alexis.

"Thanks. He got them for me for my birthday—a week late." She shook her head. "And of course he put them on my credit card. They sure are expensive these days."

"They are," Hannah said.

"But it's the thought that counts," Eric's mother said. "Anyway, there's the stuff." She pointed out a box in the corner of the living room, with a video game console and controllers. There was a stack of games next to it.

"He wants three hundred for the lot," she said.

"Wow." Jacob started plucking up the games. "There's some good stuff here. Wish I'd brought cash."

"He wants it to be a package deal," Eric's mother said. "All or nothing."

"Where is he and when will he be home?" Hannah asked.

"He went to the basketball tournament," his mother said. "It's at Hamilton High, four blocks away. He still goes to the games even though he graduated last year."

"Got it," Hannah said. "Maybe we can find him there and talk about buying the games," she said to Jacob.

"Do you know what he looks like?" asked Eric's mother doubtfully.

"Is that him?" Hannah pointed out the picture on the china hutch.

"Yep. The photo's a couple of years old but he hasn't changed much."

"Thanks for everything, Mrs. Rogers," Hannah said.

"Ms. Derringer," she corrected. "I switched back after my divorce." She showed them the door. "If you see him, tell him to come home. He posted that ad, so he should be here to meet people."

CHAPTER 8

"Well," Jacob said once they were outside. "That was cheerful."

"Seriously," Hannah said. At least now, they knew Eric hadn't lied about his name or age. And he probably wasn't after Alexis's debit card info. On the other hand . . .

"Why do you think this guy made such a sudden decision to sell off a bunch of his stuff?"

"He probably needs the money for something—maybe to buy a ring for his proposal."

Hannah grimaced. "Gross. But plausible, I guess." She thought about how Alexis was spending the day buying clothes. Thinking of her sister's expectations made Hannah's stomach hurt.

"He's been using a fake picture with Alexis," Hannah said.

"Not hard to guess why," Jacob said with a chuckle.

"Don't be mean," she said, but she knew what he meant. Eric—the real Eric—was certainly not male model material, and his sour expression didn't help. He might have a great personality, but how many girls would give him a chance? Especially online? Most would click past his picture.

No wonder he'd been calling off dates with Alexis. He was probably scared of what she would say when she finally saw him.

If he was *only* using a fake photo, that didn't make him a terrible person. But the other lies were piling up. He wasn't in college, and it didn't sound like he had a job.

They got in the car and drove a few blocks to Hamilton High School, where they saw the marquee advertising the basketball tournament.

Jacob pulled into the parking lot. "Let's go find your future brother-in-law."

"Oh, stop it," Hannah said.

The bleachers were mostly full but not packed. A team in yellow was playing a team in red, the gym echoing with the thunder of ten boys running back and forth across the floor.

She scanned the crowd. She couldn't pick out Eric.

"He's not here," said Jacob after several minutes.

"I don't think so either," said Hannah. "He lied to his mother."

"This guy sure lies a lot," Jacob said.

"Exactly," Hannah said.

They left the auditorium.

"So where is he?" Jacob asked.

"Maybe a pawnshop," Hannah guessed. "That would be a good place to find a fairly cheap engagement ring."

"But he doesn't have any money. At least he won't until someone buys his stuff."

"He could be pawning something in trade," she said.

"Good thought." Jacob tapped his phone and did a search. "There's a pawnshop in a strip mall a few more blocks from here."

Hannah's phone buzzed. A picture of shoes, from Alexis. They looked expensive.

Nice, she replied. But she whispered under her breath, "She's going to be crushed."

"What?" Jacob pulled into a spot at the strip mall.

"Alexis is so excited for this date. And she's spending a lot of money. And either she'll get stood up or it will be . . . well, not the Eric she's expecting."

"Yeah," said Jacob. "I feel sorry for her."

Hannah wondered if she should text Alexis the whole story, but her phone's battery icon was now just a little sliver of red. She put her phone in battery-saving mode.

The pawnshop was more crowded than Hannah had expected. There were a dozen people in the aisles, looking at everything from camping gear to musical instruments. But no Eric. Jacob went to the counter and talked to the clerk. Hannah saw Jacob gesturing, pointing at his fingers. The guy shook his head and said something. Jacob thanked the guy and came back over to Hannah.

"He said there are four or five guys a day buying or selling engagement rings."

"Really?"

"He says it's half their business. However, he doesn't think Eric was here today."

The two of them left the store and stood on the sidewalk.

"Now what?" Jacob wondered.

"Well . . ." She pointed out a store called Comics & Cards. "Maybe he's trying multiple ways to get some money."

"Maybe. Let's look."

The store was long and narrow, lined with tables that had deep boxes of comic books and flat boxes of sports cards. Eric Rogers was there, standing at the counter with a shoebox full of cards. Hannah ducked between rows of tables and watched Eric. Jacob stood across from her, flipping through the comics without even looking.

"You can't be serious," Eric was saying. "Only a hundred and eighty? For all of those?"

"Basketball cards don't appreciate the way baseball cards do," the clerk said, his hands in a "what can I do?" gesture.

"But they're in perfect condition!"

"We wouldn't buy them at all if they weren't," the clerk answered.

He's not supposed to care about sports, Hannah thought. He still went to high school basketball games and apparently collected cards. His profile was full of lies. He'd tried to put together the perfect guy: not into the same stuff as most guys, sensitive and sweet.

Eric argued his way up to two hundred dollars and the clerk took Eric's shoebox and started making out a check.

"You're giving me a check?" Eric said. "I thought it would be cash!" He tapped a sign that said "Cash for your cards."

"Not for this much at once," the clerk said. He handed Eric the check.

"I need cash! I demand that you open the register and keep your *promise* on the sign." He tapped the sign roughly, nearly knocking it to the floor.

"Look, we don't even have that much cash," the clerk said. He was totally unfazed. Maybe comic book people were always throwing tantrums in his store. "And if you make a scene I'll call the police."

"Sorry." Eric sighed, folded the check and put it in his wallet. As he did, he seemed to notice that the other customers in the store had seen his outburst, and he looked down, embarrassed. He walked out without another word, making the bell jangle.

The clerk nodded at Hannah and Jacob. "Let me know if you need help finding anything!"

"We're good," said Jacob. They spent another minute browsing, then left. They saw Eric heading into the pawnshop and followed him. As Hannah stepped back into the shop, she saw Eric at the glass case with jewelry.

He was buying a ring after all. She felt like she was going to faint. It made everything so real. By the end of the night, Alexis would have that ring on her finger. And Eric would probably tell her it was some kind of family heirloom.

He turned and saw her. His eyes narrowed. She wheeled around and left, Jacob right behind her.

"So what do we do now?" he asked.

"We need to go home," said Hannah. "I have to tell Alexis everything—before she goes to meet him."

"Can we go to that donut shop first?" Jacob pointed at one across the parking lot. "I love their donuts."

"Sure," Hannah sighed. "My treat."

/////

Jacob put away two donuts before she finished one. "I forgot to have lunch," he said around a full mouth. Hannah remembered her sandwich. It was hard to believe it was the same day. So much had happened in the last few hours.

"Guess who's here," Jacob whispered, spraying crumbs on the table. Hannah glanced at the counter and saw Eric. He bought a coffee and poured three little plastic cups of cream into it before he sat down. He pulled a jewelry box out of his pocket, opened it and peeked inside, then snapped it shut and put it in his pocket. He was sweating even though it was wintery cold outside.

Hannah reached for her phone but remembered that it was almost dead.

"Take his picture," she whispered.

"What?"

"I need to take his photo and send it to Alexis."

"Um. OK." Jacob took out his phone and opened the camera. He pretended he'd flipped the camera to the front and was taking a selfie. He even threw an arm around Hannah and grinned. She played along, leaned in and smiled. Jacob moved the camera until Eric was in the frame, and snapped the photo. Unfortunately, the late afternoon sun was shining through the window behind Eric, casting a dark shadow.

The camera sensed the darkness and flashed. Hannah's heart dropped.

Eric noticed the flash and raised his eyebrows. He stood up and started heading toward their table.

"Did you just take my photo?" He seemed so much bigger than before.

"No," said Jacob. "Why would we?"

"I keep seeing you two. Comic store, pawnshop. Now here." He didn't outright accuse them of following him or spying on him, but his face was full of suspicion. "What's going on?"

"We were here first," Jacob pointed out. "Maybe you're following us."

Eric seemed to think it over. "OK, then. Let me see the picture."

"No." Jacob stood up to face him.

Eric was a head taller. What would Jacob do? Throw a donut at him?

"I mean, I can't. I deleted it. It didn't look good."

Eric looked like he might make trouble, but his own phone buzzed. He glanced at it, then hurried back to his table, tapping out a reply.

"What just happened?" Jacob whispered.

"I think Alexis just texted him."

"Good timing," he said. "We should get out of here."

"Yeah. Let's get back to Mason Falls before he does," Hannah said. "We have to warn Alexis."

CHAPTER 9

They didn't talk much on the drive home. Hannah was too lost in her own thoughts, playing out all the ways she could break the truth to Alexis.

Jacob dropped her off at home.

"Thanks again for doing all this," she said. "I'll let you know when I have an update."

"It was my pleasure. Um, can we go out sometime?" he blurted. "When we're not spying on anyone?"

"Absolutely," she said.

He waited until she got inside before he drove away.

He's a good guy, Hannah thought. She didn't know if she liked him the way Alexis liked imaginary Eric, but at least she knew who he really was.

/////

The shower was running when Hannah went upstairs. Eventually Alexis came out, one towel wrapped around her body and another around her hair, and sprinted to her room.

Hannah waited for the blow dryer to go off before she tapped on Alexis's door.

"Come in."

Hannah pushed open the door. Alexis was almost dressed. Black jeans and her new blouse. Nice, but not like she was trying too hard. It was perfect.

Alexis held one set of earrings up to her ears, then another. She looked at Hannah. "Which should I wear?"

"The sea shells," Hannah replied instinctively. "They sort of match the shirt."

"Smart." Alexis put them in. She went to the bureau and started on her makeup.

"So obviously the date is still on," Hannah said.

"Of course," said Alexis. "I mean, as far as I know. He hasn't checked in in a while, but he does have a long drive."

Not that long, Hannah thought.

"Are you scared?" she asked. "Since you've never met him in person?" She had so much to tell her sister, but didn't know where to begin.

"Not really," Alexis said. She applied lipstick. "I mean, I feel like I know him so well."

You don't though. Hannah felt like she would burst. "Actually, I kind of did a little research on Eric," she said. "And it turns out that's not his picture. And he's not actually in college."

Alexis stared at her in astonishment. "And how do you know all this?"

"Because we found him."

"Who is we?" said Alexis, confused.

"Jacob and me. We drove to Eric's house, which is not in Silver Valley. He lives with his mom and plays video games all day. He doesn't have a job. He's selling all of his stuff just to go on this date."

"Really?" Alexis seemed more touched than angry. "What did he sell?"

"Sports cards. By the way, he likes sports. Especially basketball. Which is another thing he's lied to you about," she pointed out.

"Everybody fudges the truth a little early in a relationship," Alexis said.

"But he lied about being in college!" Hannah burst out.

"Are you sure he's not? Maybe he doesn't go to the U, but he could go to a community college or a satellite campus." She snapped her fingers. "Online classes, even."

"I guess you could be right," Hannah admitted. "But his mother says . . ."

"You met his *mom*?" Alexis's mouth hung open, shiny red with lipstick.

"I didn't plan on it!"

"Hannah, that is so weird and wrong and I don't have time for it. Please go away," Alexis snapped at her, reaching for the mascara.

"But Alexis, you can't go through with this date!" Hannah cried, trying not to show her panic.

"Why not? Because if he likes basketball and isn't in college he's a bad person?" She flipped the little brush across her lashes. Hannah was impressed. She couldn't put on mascara without making a mess of it, and her sister could do it in the middle of an argument.

Hannah tried one last argument. "He also seems really short-tempered. He almost started a fight with Jacob."

"Probably because you were stalking him!" Alexis snapped the mascara case back together and dropped it on the dresser.

"Well, he makes me uncomfortable," said Hannah.

"I've had bad dates before, Hannah. I don't need my baby sister to save me." She stood up and waved her out of the room.

"Alexis . . ." Hannah started. "At least let me go with you."

"What? You cannot be serious!" Alexis looked horrified at the thought.

"I am serious. Let me go with you." Hannah really hated what she was about to say, but she couldn't think of any other way. She had to play her final card. "Let me go or I'm telling Mom."

///////

It was a cold night, but it felt even colder inside the car as Alexis drove downtown. Alexis was *not* happy.

Hannah sat in the passenger seat, wishing she'd had a chance to recharge her phone. She wanted to send Jacob updates.

Alexis pulled into the parking lot of an Italian restaurant. It was one of the fancier places in Mason Falls. She tried to storm across the parking lot, but it was nearly impossible to walk in heels on icy blacktop. She slipped and Hannah swooped in to stop her from falling. Alexis muttered a thank you.

"So are you going to chaperone the whole dinner?" Alexis asked when they were seated.

"After you meet him, if you want me to go, just give me a nudge. I'll go to a movie or something."

"Fine."

They ate breadsticks and drank water for an hour before Eric finally arrived, wearing a jacket that was too tight and pants that were too short. Alexis looked at him in confusion.

Eric stepped forward. "It's me," he said.

"But . . ."

"I know I'm not as handsome as you thought. I'll explain."

"Oh, you're plenty handsome." Alexis stood up and traded kisses on the cheek. Hannah wasn't sure if Alexis meant it or was just being nice.

Eric sat down, then stood again and removed his jacket. Hannah pretended to look at a menu, hoping he wouldn't even notice her.

"It's warm," he said. The chair squeaked as he moved it to sit again.

"It is warm," Alexis agreed, even though it wasn't. Just awkward and tense.

Eric dabbed at his forehead with his shirt cuffs. "I know I'm not the guy you've seen," he said. "I used another photo for my profile, because . . . well, I wasn't that serious about it at first. I wasn't really expecting to meet anyone. Especially someone like you." He gave Alexis a searching look.

"It's fine," said Alexis with a fake laugh. "My picture doesn't look like me either."

"It does. I mean, you're lovelier in real life, but your photo looks like you."

Hannah suppressed the urge to roll her eyes. Eric finally noticed her and did a double take.

"I'm the baby sister," she said matter-of-factly.

"Oh. Hi." He obviously recognized her from the donut shop. Hannah gave him a hard stare.

Eric took a deep breath and turned back to Alexis. "I might as well tell you, I'm not really in college," he said in a rush. "I'm applying to go next year, and I really am going to major in business. Everything else I told you is true. I faked some of the information on the profile because I wanted to look good, and once we got talking, I kept thinking, I have to come clean. But I was afraid you would stop talking to me."

"Oh," said Alexis slowly. "Well, I—I don't know if I'm OK with this to be honest. It seems like—like our whole relationship is based on false pretenses." The waiter was headed their way. Hannah shook her head at him. *Not a good time.* He nodded and walked away.

"Look," said Eric. "If I'd posted my real photo and had told the truth about college, would you have talked to me at all? Would you have gotten to know me?"

Hannah winced. He was making Alexis seem shallow.

"Maybe not," Alexis admitted. "But I have a right to know who I'm talking to." Her voice was stern and steady now.

"I know," Eric said. "Listen, I wanted to come clean for so long. Fibbing on the profile felt harmless. I never expected it to go this far . . ." He reached for his water again, for something to do. He sipped noisily, then put the glass down. "Anyway, I'm telling you now. Coming one hundred percent clean. No more lies. Do you still want to do this?"

"Dinner? Or all of it?"

"Dinner for starters," he said.

"Hm."

"We had all those great talks," Eric said. "That was me. It's not like I can make that up."

"I know. You were always sweet on the phone," Alexis said, her voice softening. For the first time, Alexis looked at him like she *might* still like him. Hannah was frozen to her seat. She felt like she was watching a slow motion train wreck. *Alexis can't still want to go through with this, right?*

"You haven't lied about anything else?" Alexis asked, her stern voice returning. "Your car breaking down?"

"It was my mom's car, but yeah. I was really planning on meeting you that week."

"What about the flu?"

"I wish I was lying about that. It was awful."

"Hmm." Alexis considered him carefully. "What do you think, Hannah?"

"Me?" *Suddenly you want my opinion?* She turned to Eric. Maybe he wasn't a bad guy, but he was still lying about so much. He'd tricked his mother into paying for the flowers. He pretended to be into the same things as Alexis, but he was all about basketball and video games. Who even knew where it ended?

I wonder what he'd do if I asked about what happened at the donut shop, thought Hannah. *If he lies to me, maybe Alexis will finally see through his charm.* "You know, you look familiar," she told Eric. "Have we met?"

He looked at her a long time, like he was studying her face and trying to recall. But obviously he recognized her from earlier that day. Hannah hadn't even changed clothes! She realized he was trying to figure out what *she* wanted him to say. He wasn't thinking about simply telling the truth. He was calculating.

"I don't think so," he said at last.

"Funny you don't remember her," Alexis said. "Since she followed you around all day and you practically got in a fight with her friend. I can't believe you're still lying to me." She sounded furious. She waved at the waiter, who quickly came over.

"Dinner is off," she told the waiter. "Can I pay for the bread?"

"No need," he said. "Sorry things didn't work out."

Alexis started for the door. Hannah wondered if she'd leave *both* of them behind. She hurried to catch up. Eric walked behind them, muttering apologies.

Hannah turned back and offered a forced smile. "Hope you get your cards back," she said.

"Huh? Oh. Yeah. I think . . . maybe I'll try."

Alexis stopped at the door.

"Come on, Hannah!"

CHAPTER 10

"Why didn't you stop me from doing this?" Alexis said the moment Hannah was in the car. "He is such a loser. He's hopeless!"

"I tried!" Hannah protested.

"I know, I know. But I feel like such an idiot!"

"No!" said Hannah. "You're the smartest person I know. But he was probably charming online. And on the phone."

"Still. You saw right through him and I didn't."

"I'm good at not trusting people," Hannah said.

"Maybe that's the student group you'll form," Alexis said. She started the car. "The We Don't Trust Anybody Club."

"Imagine trying to get elected treasurer of that club," Hannah said.

They both laughed long and hard. It felt good. At last, Alexis backed out of their parking spot.

"I'm still hungry," she said. "You?"

"Starving!"

"Let's go somewhere that's cheaper." Alexis started driving toward the mall. "You know what? It was never about him," she said, thinking aloud. "I got carried away by this fantasy where I didn't have to grow up and go to college. I could just put it all on hold for a while. Maybe live on a beach."

"You can still do that," said Hannah. "I mean, at least the college part."

Alexis parked near the same café where Hannah had had lunch. Hannah couldn't believe it was the same day. The longest, craziest day ever. On top of everything else, hadn't a pretty good guy asked her out on a date? She'd barely thought about it in the blizzard of worrying about Alexis.

"When we get home I have to tell Mom about the gap year," Alexis said after they were seated. "I guess I don't want to live that lie anymore either."

"That's a good idea," said Hannah. She ordered a hamburger. Alexis, being Alexis, ordered a dinner salad. But when the waitress asked if they wanted dessert, she got a gleam in her eye.

"Do you want pie?"

"Always," said Hannah. "Key lime," she said to the waitress.

"Pecan for me," Alexis said.

The waitress scribbled down their order and disappeared.

"Tell Mom you're eloping with some guy," Hannah suggested. "Then when she finds out you really aren't, the gap year won't seem so bad."

"Ha. Very funny. Han, I'm sorry I was so mad at you. You were just looking out for me."

"Thanks. I mean, I'm sorry I went behind your back to find out more about Eric. But I *was* trying to look out for you, and I'm glad you're not mad at me."

The waitress brought them their pie.

Hannah dug into her piece with enthusiasm, and so did Alexis.

Alexis took the check when the waitress came back.

"It's on me," she said. "Oh, but can you bring us two slices of apple to go?"

"Bringing pie for Mom and Wayne?" Hannah wondered.

"It's for breakfast tomorrow," Alexis said, smiling. "For both of us."

ABOUT THE AUTHOR

Israel Keats was born and raised in North Dakota and now lives in Minneapolis. He is fond of dogs and national parks.